Stories of Pirates

Russell Punter

Illustrated by
Christyan Fox

Reading Consultant: Alison Kelly
Roehampton University

Contents

Chapter 1

The pesky parrot 3

Chapter 2

Captain Spike 22

Chapter 3

The Masked Pirate 31

The pesky parrot

It was Charlie Crossbones' first day as a pirate.

He'd spent the last ten years at Pirate School. Now he was ready to set sail for treasure.

He knew how to...

read a
treasure
map...

unlock a
chest...

...and do lots of
other piratey
things.

4

He even knew how to give a proper pirate's laugh.

What's more, Charlie had been lucky enough to inherit his Grandpa's old pirate ship and all the gear to go with it.

But as Charlie looked at his outfit, he realized something was missing. He didn't have a parrot.

A moment later, Charlie spotted just what he needed.

USED PARROT SALE

Get the bird here!

Parrots going cheap!

There were parrots of all shapes and sizes. There was only one problem. They were all too expensive.

As Charlie turned to go, the parrot seller called him back. "I suppose you could have this one," he said.

Charlie had never seen such a pretty parrot and he was amazed it was so cheap.

Now he had his parrot, Charlie wasted no time in setting off on his hunt for treasure.

9

Out at sea, Charlie spotted a ship called the *Fat Flounder*. He knew it belonged to a rich sailor called Captain Silverside.

Charlie waited until the sailors had gone to lunch. Then he rowed across to the ship and sneaked in through an open window.

Charlie was in luck. He'd climbed into the cabin where the captain kept his treasure.

But he had only just begun to stuff his pockets with gold coins, when disaster struck.

"Sssh!" Charlie hissed at his parrot. But it was too late.

Charlie took one look at
Captain Silverside
and ran.

COME BACK HERE,
YOU SNEAKY THIEF!

The
captain
and his
men chased
Charlie around
the deck six times before the
poor pirate escaped to his boat.

13

As he rowed back to his ship, Charlie turned to his parrot with a face like thunder.

But every time they went to sea, the parrot caused trouble.

Just as Charlie was about to steal someone's treasure, the parrot let out a warning cry.

Each time, Charlie only just managed to escape. Soon, he was a nervous wreck. Whenever he tried to get rid of the parrot...

...it always found its way back to Charlie's shoulder.

16

As Charlie was eating
his supper one evening, he
wondered what he could do.

The Laughing Lobster Inn

Super Deluxe Menu

Scrummy Scampi   7 pennies
Mouthwatering Mussels   6 pennies

Deluxe Menu

Crispy Cod   5 pennies
Fancy Fishcakes   4 pennies

Cheap Menu

Shrimp on toast   2 pennies

Very Cheap Menu

Bread & cheese   1 penny

He had never felt so
miserable. Thanks to that
pesky parrot he was a useless,
practically penniless pirate.

Charlie's long face was making the other customers lose their appetites. The landlord tried to cheer him up.

They were so busy talking, neither of them spotted a thief creeping up to the landlord's cash box.

The thief was just about to swipe all the money, when Charlie's parrot squawked into action.

"What a wonderful bird!"
said the landlord. "That thief
nearly got away with my
cash."

This gave Charlie an idea.
Perhaps he could put his
parrot to good use after all.

The landlord paid Charlie
handsomely for his new
burglar alarm...

STOP THIEF!

the parrot
enjoyed its
new job...

...and Charlie
had enough
money to buy
another bird –
a quiet one this
time.

Chapter 2

Captain Spike

Macintosh Mullet was a poor fisherman. He lived on tiny Mullet Island with only his daughter, Molly, for company.

One winter, the weather was so bad that Macintosh didn't catch a single fish.

So, Molly put her father's telescope, her best blue vase and a china cat into a wooden chest and set off for the mainland.

Molly had been rowing for ten minutes when she was spotted by Captain Spike and his band of pirates.

In a flash, they dragged her and the chest on board.

The mean captain tried
everything to
make
Molly
talk...

Yuck!

...but she
wouldn't
give him
the key.

"Then I'll smash the chest
open!" he cried. As he spoke, a
thick fog came down around
the ship.

"Help!" cried the pirate who was steering. "I can't see!"

"I know these seas," said Molly. "Promise to let me go, and I'll guide you home."

"Hmm... OK," said Spike. "Shark Island, and step on it!"

An hour passed and the fog began to clear a little.

"I'll take over now," said Spike. "I can't have other pirates see you steer my ship, I'd be a laughing stock."

"Can I go then?" asked Molly.
"No!" said Spike, with a sneer.
"You can walk the plank!"

The sneaky captain had broken his promise. Leaving one of his crewmen at the wheel, Spike forced Molly to walk to the end of a plank, into the shark-filled sea below.

But there was no splash... not even a tiny splish. All the pirates heard was a thud!

At that moment, the fog
cleared as quickly as it had
sprung up.

"This isn't Shark Island!"
growled Spike. "She's tricked
us. Quick lads! Out of here."

It was too late. Before the pirates could move, the port police jumped on board. Soon, Spike and his men were safely behind bars.

But the port police were still worried about the fog. So they built a lighthouse next to Mullet Island and made Molly the lighthouse keeper.

Chapter 3

The Masked Pirate

Sam Sardine had always wanted to be a sailor.

He was desperate to travel the Seven Seas and do battle with bloodthirsty pirates.

As soon as he was old enough, he joined Captain Winkle's ship as a cabin boy.

But Sam soon found that life on board ship wasn't as exciting as he'd thought.

He spent all day...

mopping
the decks...

peeling
potatoes...

...and
washing
the sailors'
smelly
socks.

33

Finally, he'd had enough.
He went to the captain and
asked for a proper sailor's job.

Captain Winkle thought Sam
was rather rude. But he decided
to put him to the test.

"All right," he said, "Let's see
you sail the ship into port!"

Sam's chest swelled with pride as he took the wheel.

But steering a ship wasn't as easy as it looked.

Luckily, the ship wasn't too badly damaged. Sam begged for one more chance.

"Very well," said Captain Winkle, at last. "You can guard the ship's treasure."

That night,
while the rest
of the sailors
snored in their
bunks,
Sam sat
guard.

But he was
exhausted after his
hard day's
work.
Soon, he
was fast
asleep
as well.

ZZZ..!

Hours later, Sam was woken from his dreams by a wicked laugh.

He rushed up on deck, to see the dreaded Masked Pirate sailing off with Captain Winkle's treasure.

Sam felt terrible. What would the captain say? He didn't have to wait long to find out.

When Captain Winkle had calmed down, he offered a reward to whoever could track down the thief or his treasure.

But, as the pirate always
wore a mask, no one knew
what he looked like.
Suddenly, Sam had an idea.

Captain Winkle didn't have much confidence in his cabin boy, but no one else had a plan.

That evening, Sam went to the Spyglass Inn, where the local pirates spent the night.

At breakfast next morning, Sam said in a loud voice, "I heard the Masked Pirate talking in his sleep last night."

He described the spot where he hides his treasure!

One particular pirate sitting in a corner began to look worried. Sam's plan was working.

"Now I know where the treasure is, I'm going to get it for myself!" Sam went on.

Hearing this, the pirate rushed out of the inn. Sam followed close behind.

The pirate jumped into a boat and rowed to an island just off the coast.

44

Sam ran to Captain Winkle.

When they arrived
on the island, they
found the pirate
hurriedly
digging up
a treasure
chest.

The captain recognized it at once. It was *his* treasure chest. Taking a flying leap, he landed on the pirate.

"Take my ship and fetch help, Sam my boy!" he roared.

"You trust me to sail?" cried Sam. "Aye aye, Captain!"

There are lots more great stories for you to read:

Usborne Young Reading: Series One
Aladdin and his Magical Lamp
Animal Legends
Stories of Dragons
Stories of Giants
Stories of Gnomes & Goblins
Stories of Magical Animals
Stories of Princes & Princesses
Stories of Witches
The Burglar's Breakfast
The Dinosaurs Next Door
The Monster Gang
Wizards

Usborne Young Reading: Series Two
A Christmas Carol
Aesop's Fables
Gulliver's Travels
Jason & The Golden Fleece
Robinson Crusoe
The Adventures of King Arthur
The Amazing Adventures of Hercules
The Amazing Adventures of Ulysses
The Clumsy Crocodile
The Fairground Ghost
The Incredible Present
Treasure Island

Series editor:
Lesley Sims

This edition first published in 2007 by Usborne Publishing Ltd.,
Usborne House, 83-85 Saffron Hill, London EC1N 8RT, England.
www.usborne.com Copyright © 2007, 2003 Usborne Publishing Ltd.